KIDS' SPORTS

LACROSSE FIELD BLUNDERS

by Dionna L. Mann

illustrated by Amanda Erb

PICTURE WINDOW BOOKS
a capstone imprint

Published by Picture Window Books, an imprint of Capstone
1710 Roe Crest Drive, North Mankato, Minnesota 56003
capstonepub.com

Library of Congress Cataloging-in-Publication Data
Names: Mann, Dionna L., author. | Erb, Amanda, illustrator.
Title: Lacrosse field blunders / Dionna L. Mann ; [illustrator, Amanda Erb]
Other titles: Kids' sports stories.
Description: North Mankato, Minnesota : Picture Window Books, an
imprint of Capstone, [2022] | Series: Kids' sports stories | Includes
bibliographical references. | Audience: Ages 5-7. | Audience: Grades K-1. |
Summary: Myra encourages her best friend, Myra, to try out for the
lacrosse team, and although she is not really good at sports, Gabi allows
herself to be persuaded; but when she struggles in a game Myra gets mad
at her, and blames her for the loss--and the two friends realize they have
to work at being not just friends, but true teammates.
Identifiers: LCCN 2021023341 (print) | LCCN 2021023342 (ebook) |
ISBN 9781663959355 (hardcover) | ISBN 9781666331264 (paperback) |
ISBN 9781666331271 (ebook pdf) Subjects: LCSH: Lacrosse--Juvenile
fiction. | Teamwork (Sports)—Juvenile fiction. | Best friends—Juvenile
fiction. | Helping behavior—Juvenile fiction. | CYAC: Lacrosse—Fiction. |
Teamwork (Sports)—Fiction. | Best friends—Fiction. | Friendship—Fiction. |
Helpfulness—Fiction. | LCGFT: Sports fiction.
Classification: LCC PZ7.1.M3659 Lac 2022 (print) | LCC PZ7.1.M3659
(ebook) | DDC [E]—dc23 LC record available at https://lccn.loc.
gov/2021023341 LC ebook record available at https://lccn.loc.
gov/2021023342

Editorial Credits
Editor: Carrie Sheely; Designer: Bobbie Nuytten; Media Researcher:
Morgan Walters; Production Specialist: Laura Manthe

Printed and bound in the United States of America. PO4608

TABLE OF CONTENTS

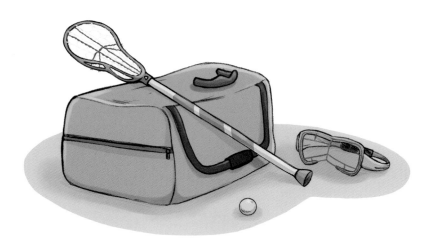

Glossary

assist—when one player makes a move that directly results in a teammate scoring a goal

blog—a website used to share articles that are usually written by one person or a small group of people

cradle—to keep the ball inside the lacrosse stick's net, or pocket, when running

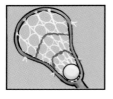
draw—when two players face each other in the center of the field and the ball is held firmly between both sticks; when the players quickly move their sticks up, the ball is released and each team fights to get the ball

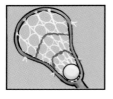
pocket—the netted part of the lacrosse stick

Chapter 1

TRYOUTS

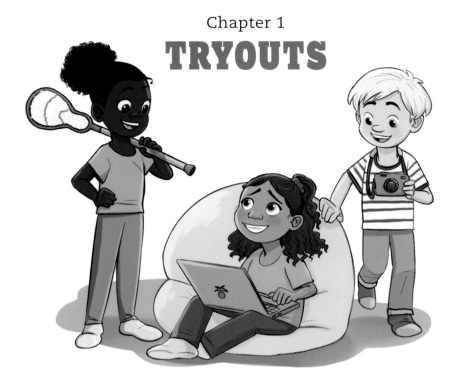

"Are you coming to lacrosse tryouts?" Myra asked her best friend, Gabi.

"I think I'll stick to writing for my **blog**," Gabi said.

"Playing lacrosse is fun!" Myra said.

"I don't know," Gabi said. "I'm not very good at sports."

"Go for it, Gabi!" Gabi's cousin Zach said. Then he went back to taking photos for Gabi's blog.

"Please, try out for the team," said Myra. "We'll get to spend more time together."

"It looks hard," Gabi said.

"I can show you what to do," Myra said. "Let's go down to the field."

The girls got to the field just in time for tryouts. Myra ran. Her ball danced inside the net, or **pocket,** of her lacrosse stick. The ball soared across the field when Myra threw it.

"See," Myra said. "Easy peasy. I know you can do it too!"

Gabi could see how happy it would make Myra if she tried out. And she did like to learn new things.

"Okay, I'll try out," Gabi said.

"WOO-HOO!" Myra shouted.

After tryouts, Myra and Gabi walked home. "That was kind of fun," Gabi said.

"Just think!" Myra said. "If you make it on the team, you'll be part of a team that never loses."

"Never?" Gabi replied.

"Never!" Myra said.

Gabi began to worry. "Maybe it would be best if I didn't make it."

"You'll be great. You're my friend, after all," Myra said.

Chapter 2
OUT OF THE POCKET

A couple days later, Coach called to tell Gabi she was on the team. At first, Gabi was happy. But after a few practices, Gabi felt unsure. When she tried to **cradle** the ball, it always rolled away. And a game was coming up.

What if I let down Myra? Gabi thought.

When game day arrived, Gabi was
nervous.

"What's wrong, Gabi?" asked Myra.

Gabi looked down. "Oh, I'm fine. Just game-day jitters."

"Shake it off. We need you today!" said Myra.

Soon, Coach put Gabi in the game. When she got the ball and ran, she lost it. After someone passed it to her later, she lost it again.

Myra squinted at Gabi. "Will you try to keep hold of the ball?"

Gabi gulped. She was trying.

During the break, Zach walked up to Gabi. "Want to see the pics?" he asked.

"Delete the ones with me," Gabi said.

Zach saw Myra shoot an annoyed look at Gabi.

"What's with Myra?" Zach asked.

"She thinks it's my fault we're losing," Gabi said. "I'm awful."

"You're playing hard and still learning," Zach said. "Just do your best!"

It was time for the second half to begin.

"For the **draw**," Coach said, "Gabi's up."

"But Dad," Myra said, "we're already down three points!"

Coach gave Myra a look.

"Choose someone else. It's okay," Gabi said.

"No," Coach said. "Everyone gets a turn."

Myra stomped off the field.

Gabi got ready for the draw. The ball flew up.

Gabi caught it! She started to run.

Then Gabi's ball rolled out of the pocket
and out of play.

The game ended in a loss.

"It's your fault!" Myra yelled at Gabi.

Coach gathered the team. "Remember, a good team works together. A good player helps her teammates. That's more important than winning."

Myra looked at the ground.

A teammate said, "Don't worry, Gabi. You'll get better."

Gabi wasn't sure. Would Myra still be her friend if she didn't get better soon?

Chapter 3

SWEET ASSIST

During school lunch on Monday, Myra sat next to Gabi. "About Saturday . . . " Myra started.

"I know. I messed up," Gabi said.

"No, I did. I'm sorry I yelled at you," Myra said.

"It's okay," Gabi replied. "I wish lacrosse was easier for me."

"I don't understand," said Myra. "I just get the ball and play. It seems so easy for me."

"Is anything hard for you?" Gabi asked.

Myra thought about it. "Writing."

"Really? I just grab my pen and write," Gabi said.

They laughed.

"I'll help you with lacrosse," Myra said.

"I'll help you with writing," Gabi said.

Over the next week, the girls helped each other. Gabi helped Myra make her writing more interesting.

Myra helped Gabi learn how to cradle the ball. She showed her how to move her wrists. She showed her how to sway the stick.

Gabi was less nervous for the next game.

The game started. When the ball came toward Gabi, she caught it. She ran. The ball stayed in the pocket! She passed it. Myra caught it and scored a point!

"Sweet **assist**!" Coach yelled.

Gabi was proud. She and Myra had played well together. This time, the team won!

Myra ran over to Gabi. "You're the best!"

"I'm getting better," Gabi said, "but I'm not the best."

"Yes, you are. You're the best at being my friend!" Myra said.

MAKE A LEVER

When Myra throws the ball to make the winning point, her arm moves like a lever. A lever is a simple machine that makes lifting loads easier. Make a lever called a catapult using household objects.

What You Need:
- ruler
- glue stick
- eraser

What You Do:
- Lay the glue stick on a table. Place the ruler on top of the glue stick. The middle of the ruler should be resting on the glue stick.
- Place one end of the ruler down on the table, and put the eraser on that end.
- With your other hand, push down sharply on the other end of the ruler.
- Watch the eraser fly!

Take another look at this illustration. Do you think it took courage for Myra to say she was sorry? Can you think of something you said or did that might have hurt someone you care about? Try writing an apology. Be sure to take ownership of what you said or did that might have hurt them.

ABOUT THE AUTHOR

Dionna L. Mann is a children's book author and freelance journalist who in her younger days loved biking, swimming, jogging, and meandering through the woods. She spent more than 25 years volunteering and working in the school system where her talented now-grown children attended. Her favorite part of working with children was teaching them about the writing process and reading the beautiful and heartfelt words they penned. As a person of color, she enjoys learning about lesser-known people found in the records of African American history. One day she hopes to swim with dolphins. You can find her online at dionnalmann.com.

ABOUT
THE ILLUSTRATOR

Amanda Erb is an illustrator from Maryland currently living in the Boston, Massachusetts, area. She earned a BFA in illustration from Ringling College of Art and Design. In her free time, she enjoys playing soccer, learning Spanish, and discovering new stories to read.